Little Sister, Big Sister

Here are some other
Redfeather Chapter Books
you will enjoy:

~~~

The Friendship of Milly and Tug
by Dian Curtis Regan
illustrated by Jennifer Danza

Hot Fudge Hero
by Pat Brisson
illustrated by Diana Cain Bluthenthal

Marty Frye, Private Eye
by Janet Tashjian
illustrated by Laurie Keller

Little Sister, Big Sister

Pat Brisson

illustrated by
Diana Cain Bluthenthal

a redfeather chapter book

Henry Holt and Company

New York

For Mary Beth McDonough and Kathy Maleski,
my big sisters
—P. B.

Lovingly dedicated to big brother Cameron
and his new little sister or brother . . .
—D. C. B.

Henry Holt and Company, Inc.
Publishers since 1866
115 West 18th Street
New York, New York 10011

Henry Holt is a registered trademark of Henry Holt and Company, Inc.

Library of Congress Cataloging-in-Publication Data
Brisson, Pat. Little sister, big sister / by Pat Brisson; illustrated by
Diana Cain Bluthenthal. p. cm. (A redfeather chapter book)
Summary: Hester and her younger sister, Edna, play Queen and her
maid, pretend to be mermaids, eat chocolate, and experience a thunderstorm.
[1. Sister—Fiction.] I. Bluthenthal, Diana Cain, ill. II. Title. III. Series.
PZ7.B78046Li 1999 [Fic]—dc21 98-33905

ISBN 0-8050-5887-7 / First Edition—1999
Printed in Mexico
1 3 5 7 9 10 8 6 4 2

Contents

Little Sister, Big Sister

Queen

It was summer.
The morning sun poured
through Hester's window.
Hester looked around her room.
She looked at her desk.
She looked at her bed.
She looked at the floor.
Her mother was right.
This room was a mess.
And she could not go out
to play with her friends
until it was all cleaned up.

Hester hated cleaning her room.
She hated hanging up her clothes.
She hated making her bed.
And she really hated picking up
her puzzles and crayons and toys
and putting them all away.

She looked at the mess
and felt sorry for herself.
Then her little sister, Edna, walked in.
She was holding her doll, Agnes,
and singing her a song.
Hester got an idea.

"Hey, Edna, do you want
to play a game?
I just made it up.
It's called Queen."
"How do you play it?" Edna asked,
rocking Agnes in her arms.
"It's easy," said Hester.
"One of us is the Queen
and one of us is the maid.
The Queen sits on the throne
and tells the maid what to do.

And the maid must bow
before the Queen and say,
'Yes, Your Majesty,
I wish only to serve you.'"

Edna held Agnes
up against her chest
and burped her.
"What about Agnes?
Can she play, too?"

"Oh, sure.

Agnes can be the Princess,"

Hester said.

"Well, okay," Edna agreed.

"Where do I sit?

Should the stool be my throne?"

"No, Edna.

I made up the game.

I know all the rules.

I will be Queen first
so you can see how it's played.
This will be my throne."
Hester put her pillow
in the middle of the floor.
"I will hold Princess Agnes
so you can work."
"I don't want to work, Hester.
I want to play the game."
"That's what I meant, Edna.
So, let's begin.

First, you must sort
the royal doodads,"
Hester said.
"The royal what?"
asked Edna.
"Doodads," Hester repeated.
"You know…
puzzle pieces, crayons, toys.
Then you must put them all back
where they belong.
But you must say,
'Yes, Your Majesty,
I wish only to serve you.'"

Edna handed Agnes to Hester.

"Yes, Your Majesty,

I wish only to serve you."

Hester bounced Agnes on her lap.

"You forgot to bow, Edna.

Say it again and bow this time."

"Yes, Your Majesty,

I wish only to serve you,"

Edna said,

bowing low before her sister.

Then Edna began to sort
puzzle pieces into boxes.
She put crayons
into the crayon basket.
She put toys in the toy box
and on the shelves.

"Now is it *my* turn
to be Queen?"
Edna asked her big sister
when she was all done.
"Almost," said Hester.
"But first you must put away
the royal clothing."
"Oh, all right," Edna grumbled.
"You forgot to bow again, Edna.
How can you be Queen

if you don't even know
how to be a maid?" Hester said.
"I think maybe it's easier
to be the Queen,"
Edna mumbled.

Edna put Hester's dirty socks
in the hamper.

She hung up Hester's robe
and nightgown.

She carefully closed
all the dresser drawers.

"Now it's my turn
to be Queen, Hester.
Get off the throne
and give me Princess Agnes."

Hester stood up slowly.
She looked at her room and smiled.
"Look, Edna,
even Queens work sometimes.
You can be Queen if
you help me make my bed."
"Okay," said Edna, "but first
you have to bow to me."
"Yes, Your Majesty," Hester said
as she bowed to Edna.
"I wish only to serve you."
Edna got on one side of the bed
and Hester got on the other.

They pulled the sheet tight.
They smoothed out the spread.
Then Hester picked up
the pillow from the floor.
"Wait a minute, Hester!" Edna yelled.
"That's my throne!"
"Oh, Edna,
it was just a silly game.
I don't feel like playing anymore.

I want to go out and
play with my friends," Hester said.
"But that's not fair!" shouted Edna.
"It's *my* turn to be Queen!"
"Then *be* Queen. I don't care."
Hester turned her back to Edna
and walked away.

Edna felt her eyes start to burn.
She felt two hot tears
roll down her cheeks.
She sat on the floor and hugged Agnes.

But a few minutes later
she heard Hester come back in.
Edna looked up at her big sister.
"I guess you're right, Edna.
It *is* your turn to be Queen.
What would you have me do,
Your Majesty?" Hester asked.

"You may fetch me
my royal throne," said Edna.
"And then, how about a game
of Go Fish?"
"Good idea," said Hester.
"I mean . . .
I wish only to serve you,
Your Majesty."

Edna smiled and gave
Princess Agnes a little hug.
"Oh, and one more thing, Hester."
"Yes, Your Majesty?"
Edna sat on the pillow
with Princess Agnes on her lap.
She looked at Hester and grinned.
"Don't forget to bow,"
she told her.

Mermaids

The sun was hot and high in the sky.
Edna and Hester were at the pool.
Hester held her face mask
in her hands.
Edna held her doll, Agnes,
close to her side.
Hester started for the steps.
"Let's go, Edna!
The water looks fine.
We can pretend we are mermaids."
Edna sat down on her towel
with Agnes in her lap.

She sang a song to her
and rocked her gently.
She shook her head.
"No," she told Hester.
"It looks a little too cold for Agnes.
We will go in later
when it's warmer."

After a few minutes had gone by,
Hester shouted from the pool,
"Come in, Edna.
The water isn't too cold.
We can pretend
we are mermaids
chasing dolphins in the sea."

Edna shook her head.
She turned her back
so that Agnes was in the shade.
"No," said Edna.
"Agnes doesn't like to be splashed.
We will come in later
when the splashing is over."

Hester went underwater.
She stood on her hands

and put her feet in the air.
Then she stood up again
and smiled.
"Come in the water, Edna.
We can pretend we are mermaids
doing tricks on the ocean floor."

"No," said Edna.
"Agnes is sleeping.
We will come in the water
when she wakes up."
Edna lay back on her towel.
She watched the clouds

make shapes in the sky.
Then she heard Hester shout,
"Hey! Stop that!
Give me back my mask!"

Edna sat up and looked
for Hester in the pool.
Two big kids had Hester's mask.
They were tossing it
to each other
over Hester's head.
Hester couldn't reach it.

Edna grabbed Agnes
and went to the pool.
The big kids still had
Hester's mask.
Edna wanted to help.
What could she do?

Then she had an idea.
She held Agnes high
over her head.
She took careful aim.
When the big kids threw
Hester's mask,
Edna threw Agnes.
"Go get it, Agnes!"
Edna yelled.
Agnes sailed through the air.

Bang! She hit the mask.
It plopped into the water
right in front of Hester.
Then Edna jumped in the water.
She made a huge splash
right in front of the big kids.

The big kids were surprised
by Agnes.
They were even more surprised
by Edna.
They quickly swam away
to the other end of the pool.

"Thanks for the help, Edna.
Those big kids were mean,
but you and Agnes
really surprised them."
Edna smiled at Hester.
She floated on her back
with Agnes sitting on her tummy.

"Those kids were big," Edna said.
"But they were not very smart.
Smart kids know
not to mess with mermaids."

The Chocolate Bar

Edna ran into the house.
Her doll, Agnes, was tied to her front
with a big blue scarf.
The door slammed behind them.
"Look what Mrs. Miller gave me!"
she yelled to Hester.
"A Chomper's Chewy Chocolate Bar!
Today must be my lucky day!"

"Why did she give you that?"
Hester asked.

"Agnes and I helped her
in her garden.
We pulled up big piles of weeds.
We cut down lots of dead flowers.
It took us a long time," Edna said.
"Mrs. Miller told me I was
the best helper she ever had.
She gave me this candy bar
because I worked hard."

Chomper's Chewy Chocolate Bars
were Hester's favorite.
She wished that
she had one, too.

"I thought you didn't like nuts,"
said Hester.

"Chomper's Chewy Chocolate Bars
have lots of nuts."
"I like nuts," Edna said.
"I like nuts a lot."

Edna tore the wrapper
off the top of the candy bar.
She could smell the chocolate.
"Mmmm, it *smells* good,"
she said.

"Chomper's Chewy Chocolate Bars
stick to your teeth, Edna.
What would Dr. Rose say?
You know too much candy
is not good for your teeth,"
Hester said.
"One candy bar is not too much,"
Edna answered.
"And I will brush my teeth
when I am done."

Edna tore off
the rest of the wrapper.
The candy bar was bumpy
where the nuts stuck out.
"Mmmm, it *looks* good, too,"
Edna said.
"It's very close to dinner, Edna.
Mom doesn't like it
when you eat close to dinner,"
Hester snapped.

"I'm so hungry,
I could eat *three*
Chomper's Chewy Chocolate Bars
and still have room for dinner,"
Edna replied.
She took a bite from one end
of her candy bar.
She closed her eyes and chewed.
"Mmmm! It *tastes* good, too,"
Edna said.

"Chocolate can melt all over
your hands, Edna.
It will make a mess
and Mom will be mad,"
Hester said.
"I will wash my hands
after I eat.

36

I will not make a mess,"
Edna said.
Edna held her
Chomper's Chewy Chocolate Bar
in her hands and
broke it into two pieces.
"Mmmm! It *feels* good, too,"
she said.
"Oh, Edna! I know
Chomper's Chewy Chocolate Bars
smell good.

I know that they *look* good.
I know that they *taste* good.
But how can a candy bar *feel* good?"
Hester shouted.

Edna smiled.
"It *feels* good
when you share it
with your sister.

Would you like some, Hester?"
Hester smiled at Edna.
"I thought you would never ask,"
she said.

Thunder Cookies

Just after dinner
the sky got dark.
The sun hid behind gray clouds.
The air felt cool.
Edna and her doll, Agnes,
were on the front sidewalk.
Edna was printing her name
with chalk.
She printed E-D-N-A
on each square of concrete
in front of her house.

Raindrops began to splash
on the sidewalk.

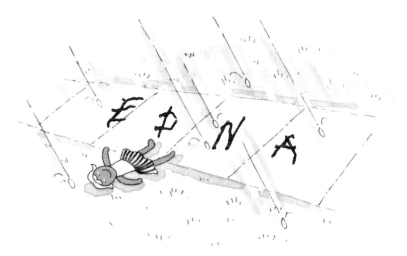

Edna picked up Agnes
and went onto the porch.
"We can sit here and
watch the rain, Agnes.
We can hear it dance on the roof.
We can watch it wash
the sidewalks clean."

But then a bright light
cut the sky.
"Lightning!" cried Edna.
CRACK! BOOM!
"And thunder!"
she said.
BOOM! CRASH!
The thunder
hurt Edna's ears.
She held Agnes close to her.
She went inside quickly.

Hester was sitting at the table
drawing pictures.
"What's the matter, Edna?
Afraid of a little thunder?"
she asked.

Edna closed the door
and looked out at the rain.
It poured off the roof.
It rushed down the street.
It soaked into the grass and dirt.
CRACK! CRASH!
The lightning streaked
across the sky.
The thunder made
Edna's tummy rumble.

"I'm a little bit afraid,"
said Edna.
The thunder boomed again.
She held Agnes tighter.
"Are you afraid, Hester?"
Hester finished her picture.
She put away her markers.

"I was afraid once.
But it's different now," Hester said.
She smiled a crooked smile
at her little sister.
"Edna, I think it's time for you
to make Thunder Cookies."
"Thunder Cookies?
What are Thunder Cookies?"
Edna asked.

Hester walked over to
the cookbook shelf.

She looked and looked.
At last she found
the book she wanted.
It was not like the others.
It was more like a notebook.
All the recipes were
written by hand.
Hester turned the pages,
looking for the right one.

"Here it is," said Hester.
"Here is the recipe for
Thunder Cookies.
I will read it to you.
You get all the things we need."

Hester read the recipe.
Edna got out nuts and raisins.
She got out oatmeal and spices.
She got out eggs and applesauce.

Then their mom came in.
Hester asked,
"Will you help us
make Thunder Cookies, Mom?"
"Oh, yes," she answered.
"Today is just right
for Thunder Cookies."
Hester, Edna, and Mom worked
for a long time.

They told jokes as they
mixed and stirred the batter.
They sang songs
as they chopped nuts.
They made up stories
as they put the cookies
onto a cookie sheet.
Outside, the thunder boomed.

Mom helped them put
the cookies in the oven.
She helped them take
the cookies out of the oven
when they were done.
Outside, the rain was ending.

"May we eat them now?"
Edna asked.

"No," said Hester.

"Thunder Cookies are special.

They are eaten in a special way.

You go wait on the porch.

We will bring them out soon."

Edna took Agnes out to the porch.

The grass and trees looked

clean and fresh.

The sky was not so gray.

The setting sun peeked

from behind a cloud.

In a little bit

Hester and Mom came out.

Hester carried the special cookbook.

Mom carried a wooden tray.

The Thunder Cookies

were on a pretty plate.

There were three fancy glasses.
And there was a blue pitcher
full of apple juice.
"Now may we eat them?"
asked Edna.

"No," Hester said.
"There is one more thing to do
before you eat Thunder Cookies."
"What is that?" Edna said.
"You must sign the
Thunder Cookie Promise.
I will read it to you."
Hester opened the cookbook and read:

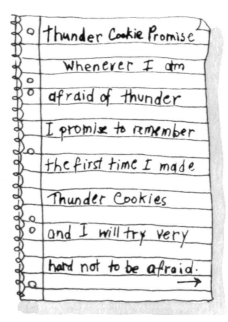

thunder Cookie Promise

Whenever I am

afraid of thunder

I promise to remember

the first time I made

Thunder Cookies

and I will try very

hard not to be afraid.
→

"See?" said Hester.

"This is where I signed the promise."

"And this is where I signed it,
a long time ago,"
said Mom.

"And this is where
Grandmom signed it,"
said Hester.

"That was a *very* long time ago."

"And now it is my turn,"
said Edna.

Edna thought about the jokes
and stories.

She thought about the songs
and the good smell of
Thunder Cookies baking.
She smiled as she wrote
E D N A
under her sister's name
in the cookbook.

"Now is it time to eat them?"
Edna asked.
Mom smiled at Edna
and kissed her cheek.
"Yes," she said,
"now it is time."

Thunder Cookies

(Please ask a grown-up to help you with this recipe.)

Cream together:
$\frac{1}{2}$ cup margarine   1 cup sugar

Add and mix well:
2 eggs   1 cup applesauce

Add to applesauce mixture and mix well:

2 cups flour	**1 teaspoon baking soda**
2 cups oatmeal	**1 teaspoon cinnamon**
1 teaspoon salt	**$\frac{1}{2}$ teaspoon ground cloves**

Stir in:
1 cup raisins
1 cup walnut pieces

Drop by rounded teaspoonfuls onto greased cookie sheets.
Bake at 350 degrees for 10 to 12 minutes or until done.
Makes 4 $\frac{1}{2}$ to 5 dozen cookies.

Do you see the bumps made by the raisins and walnuts?
That's the thunder!

J   Brisson, Pat.

           Little sister, big
           sister.

$15.95

		DATE	11 99